Yellow

ቢጫ ቀለም

English and Amharic

Thank you to the generous team who gave their time
and talents to make this book possible:

Author
Katie Bradley

Illustrator
Katie Bradley

Creative Directors
Caroline Kurtz, Jane Kurtz,
and Kenny Rasmussen

Translator
Worku L. Mulat

Designer
Beth Crow

Ready Set Go Books, an Open Hearts Big Dreams Project

Special thanks to Ethiopia Reads donors and staff for
believing in this project and helping get it started-- and
for arranging printing, distribution, and training in Ethiopia.

01/19/19

Yellow

ቢጫ ቀለም

English and Amharic

My best friend calls me Adey for the pretty yellow meskel flower.

በጣም የምወዳት ጓደኛዬ ውብት በተላበሰችው ቢጫ የመስቀል አበባ ተምሳሌት አደይ ብላ ትጠራኛለች።

I call her Lomi because she's like a pretty yellow lemon.

እኔም ውብቷ
የፈካ ቢጫ ሎሚ
ስለምትመስል ሎሚ
ብዬ እጠራታለሁ።

We both love
yellow.

ሁለታችንም ቢጫ
ቀለም እንወዳለን።

It is a bright, happy
and warm color.

ቢጫ ብሩህ፣ ደስ የሚልና
የሚመች ቀለም ነው።

Today as we walk to school, we look to see how many yellow things we can count.

ዛሬ ወደ ት/ቤት ስንሄድ ስንት ቢጫ ቀለማት ያላቸው ነገሮች ልንቆጥር እንደምንችል እናያለን።

Soft yellow
scarf covers
my hair.

ልስላሴ ያለው
ሻርፕ ጠጉሬን
ሸፍኗል።

One!

አንድ!

Yellow uniforms,
clean and neat.

ንጹህና የጸዱ ቢጫ
የደንብ ልብሶች።

Two!

ሁለት!

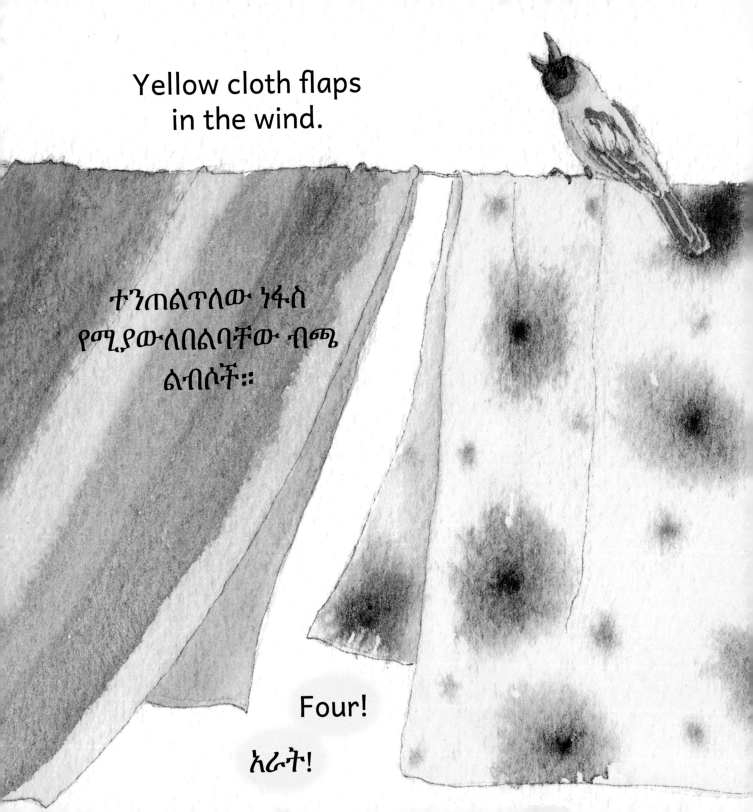

Yellow cloth flaps
in the wind.

ተንጠልጥለው ነፋስ
የሚያውለበልባቸው ብጫ
ልብሶች።

Four!

አራት!

Five!

አምስት!

Yellow birds soar
and sing.

እየዘመሩ ወደሰማይ የሚመጥቁ ቢጫ ቀለም ያላቸው ወፎች።

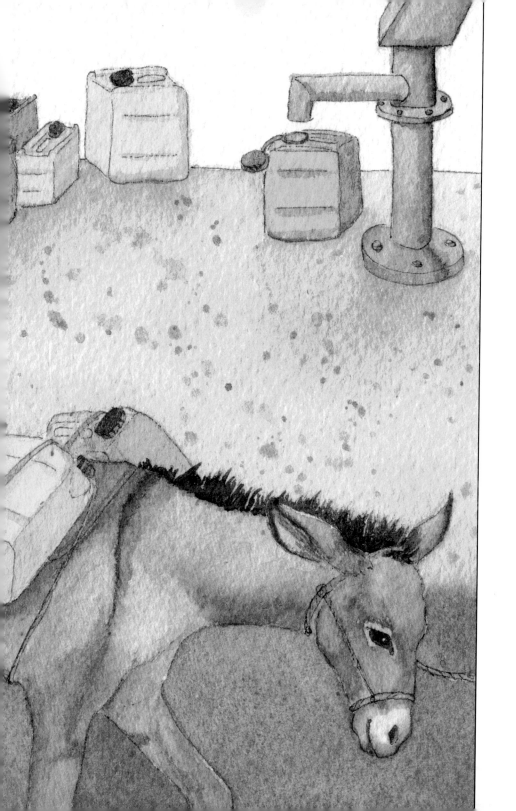

We see full jugs, too. They are heavy for the donkey to carry.

ውሃ የሞሉ ጀሪካኖችም እንመለከታለን። አህያው ለመሸከም እጅግ ከባድ ይሆኑበታል።

In the market, we see a tall roll of yellow mat.

በዘልግ ያለ የቢጫ ስጋጃ ጥቅል ገበያ ውስጥ እናያለን።

Yellow bags.

ቢጫ ሻንጣዎች።

Round yellow baskets.

ከብ ሆነው የተሠሩ ቢጫ ቅርጫቶች።

In school, we read and write. Yellow pencil, sharp and pointy.

ት/ቤት ውስጥ እናነባለን፣ እንጽፋለን። የሰላና የሾለ ቢጫ እርሳስ በመጠቀም።

Thirteen!

አሥራ ሶስት!

We eat lunch together.
Yellow split peas, spicy and good.

ምሳ አብረን እንበላለን። ብጫ አተር ክክ፣
አሳምሮ በቅመም የተሰራ።

Fourteen!

አሥራ አራት!

In the afternoon, we study mathematics.
Yellow beads slide and click.

ከሰዓት በኋላ ሂሳብ
እንማራለን። በአባከስ
ላይ የሚንሸራተቱ ቢጫ
ዶቃዎችን በመጠቀም።

Fifteen!

አሥራ አምስት!

Sixteen!

አሥራ ስድስት!

After school, we walk home. The hot yellow sun shines as we help our mothers.

ከትምህርት በኋላ ወደቤታችን እንሄዳለን። እናቶቻንን በምንረዳበት ወቅት የምታቃጥል ቢጫ ጠሃይ ትወጣብናለች።

Seventeen!

አሥራ ሰባት!

A cool yellow
moon slowly rises
as we eat dinner.

ራት በምንበላበት ወቅት ሙቀት
አልባዋ ጨረቃ ቀስ ብላ ትወጣለች።

Eighteen! አሥራ ስምንት !

The soft
yellow light
shines as
I finish my
homework.

የቤት ሥራዬን ሰርቼ
ስጨርስ መጠነኛ
የሆነው ቢጫ ብርሃን
ያርፍብኛል።

In the dark, I think of my good
day, full of many yellow things.

ሲጨልም በተለያዩ ቢጫ ቀለማት ባላቸው ነገሮች አሸበርቆ
ስለነበረው መልካም ቀን አስባለሁ፡፡ አሥራ ስምንት፡፡

Maybe tomorrow my friend and I can play
and count with our new friend.
Can you guess her nickname?

ምናልባት ነገ ጓደኛዬና እኔ ከአዲሷ ጓደኛችን ጋር እንጫወታለን፤
እንቆጥራለን...ስሟ ማን እንደሆነ መገመት ትችላለህ? ...ብርቱካን፡፡

About The Story

Harar is a fascinating city with thick, ancient walls and 368 alleys that create colorful mazes from one end to the other. Known to be the fourth most holy city of Islam, it has more than 100 mosques and shrines for people to pray in. At one time in history, the city—named a UNESCO World Heritage Site in 2016--was almost like a fortress, designed as defense against Christian neighbors. But today Muslims, Christians, and Jews live together peacefully within its walls.

In 2013, Ethiopia Reads planted a library in Model One Primary School in Harar. In 2016, a team met with school educators and 14 year-old Seada Jamal, book club coordinator, to listen to how the library is being used and share training ideas. Now Ready Set Go books will help the children of Harar practice reading in their own languages and in English.

Harar Ethiopia Reads library where children read Ready Set Go Books

About The Author and Illustrator

Katie Bradley is a mother of 3 children, one of whom was born in Ethiopia. She and her husband have traveled to Ethiopia twice, and have fallen in love with the country and its people. Amidst a busy and full life, she has become an artist and children's illustrator. Katie enjoys volunteering in her children's school and teaching art in a number of classrooms. This is her third book for Ready Set Go Books.

The inspiration for this book came while Katie Bradley and her husband were traveling from Dire Dawa to Harar, Ethiopia. She writes, "We drove past a school, and saw many children walking home. Two young girls caught my eye, walking arm in arm, both wearing yellow school uniform shirts. One girl was wearing a yellow head scarf (hijab), clearly Muslim. The other had no scarf, but had yellow earrings and a yellow cloth bag with her school supplies in it. She was wearing a necklace with a cross around her neck, identifying her as Christian. The two girls were walking with matched steps, arms looped together, laughing and talking, clearly good friends. I felt a spark of joy and hope, watching these two young women."

About Open Hearts Big Dreams

Open Hearts Big Dreams began as a volunteer organization, led by **Ellenore Angelidis** in Seattle, Washington, to provide sustainable funding and strategic support to Ethiopia reads, collaborating with **Jane Kurtz**. OHBD has now grown to be its own nonprofit organization supporting literacy, art, and technology for young people in Ethiopia.

Ellenore comes from a family of teachers who believe education is a human right, and opportunity should not depend on your birthplace. And as the adoptive mother of a little girl who was born in Ethiopia and learned to read in the U.S., as well as an aspiring author, she finds the chance to positively impact literacy hugely compelling!

About Ready Set Go Books

Reading has the power to change lives, but many children and adults in Ethiopia cannot read. One reason is that Ethiopia has very few books in local languages to give people a chance to practice reading. Ready Set Go books wants to close that gap and open a world of ideas and possibilities for kids and their communities.

When you buy a Ready Set Go book, you provide critical funding to create and distribute more books.

Learn more at: http://openheartsbigdreams.org/book-project/

Ready Set Go 10 Books

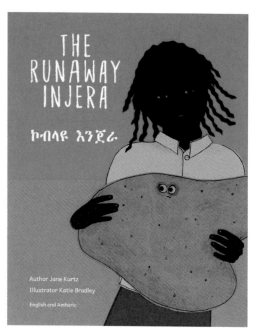

In 2018, Ready Set Go Books decided to experiment by trying a few new books in larger sizes.

Sometimes it was the art that needed a little more room to really shine. Sometimes the story or nonfiction text was a bit more complicated than the short and simple text used in most of our current early reader books.

We are calling these our "Ready Set Go 10" books as a way to show these ones are bigger and also sometimes have more words on the page. We are happy to hear feedback on these new books and on all our books.

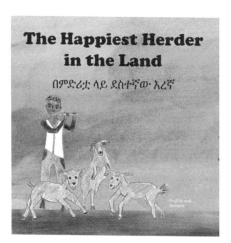

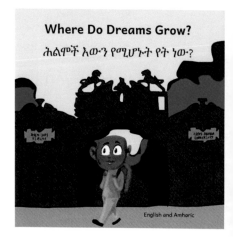

About the Language

Amharic is a Semetic language -- in fact, the world's second-most widely spoken Semetic language, after Arabic. Starting in the 12th century, it became the Ethiopian language that was used in official transactions and schools and became widely spoken all over Ethiopia. It's written with its own characters, over 260 of them. Eritrea and Ethiopia share this alphabet, and they are the only countries in Africa to develop a writing system centuries ago that is still in use today!

About the Translation

Worku L. Mulat joined the translation team of Ready Set Go Books early in 2019. He holds a PhD from University College Cork in Ireland, an MSc from Gent University, Belgium, and a BSc from Asmara University, Eritrea. Dr. Worku has published extensively professional articles on high impact journals such as Malaria Journal, Environmental Monitoring and Assessment, Ecological Indicators, Bioresource Technology, and PLOS ONE. He also co-authored three books with a main theme of Environmental conservation. Currently he is working for Open Hearts Big Dreams Fund as Innovation Center Lead in Model projects being implemented in Ethiopia. He is also a research associate at Tree Foundation which strives to save Ethiopian Orthodox church forests.

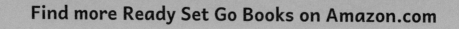

Find more Ready Set Go Books on Amazon.com

To view all available titles, search "Ready Set Go Ethiopia" or scan QR code

 Chaos

 Talk Talk Turtle

 The Glory of Gondar

 We Can Stop the Lion

 Not Ready!

 Fifty Lemons

 Count For Me

 Too Brave

 Tell Me What You Hear

Made in the USA
Middletown, DE
20 May 2019